Amelia Sparklepaw was originally
published as a Magic Animal Friends chapter
book. This version has been specially adapted
for developing readers in conjunction with a
Reading Consultant.

Special thanks to Sarah Levison

ORCHARD BOOKS

This story first published in Great Britain as
'Amelia Sparklepaw's Party Problem' in 2015 by Orchard Books
This Early Reader edition published in 2018 by The Watts Publishing Group

1 3 5 7 9 10 8 6 4 2

A CIP catalogue record for this book is available from the British Library.

ISBN 978 1 40834 591 7

Printed in China

Orchard Books
An imprint of Hachette Children's Group
Part of The Watts Publishing Group Limited
Carmelite House, 50 Victoria Embankment, London EC4Y 0DZ

An Hachette UK Company
www.hachette.co.uk
www.hachettechildrens.co.uk

Amelia Sparklepaw

Daisy Meadows

ORCHARD

www.magicanimalfriends.co.uk

Contents

PART ONE

Snapdragon Surprise

CHAPTER ONE

A Special Day

Jess Forester smiled at her best
friend, Lily Hart. "I love the
summer holidays!" Jess said.
"It means we can spend lots of
time at Helping Paw!"

The Helping Paw Wildlife
Hospital was run by Lily's
parents, and Jess lived close by.

"This sunny weather reminds me of Friendship Forest," Lily said with a smile.

Friendship Forest was a secret world full of talking animals. The girls' special friend Goldie the cat took them there by magic, for adventures.

"There's Goldie now!" Jess cried in delight.

The golden cat ran to Brightley Meadow, where the Friendship Tree stood. It looked like an old oak tree.

The girls held hands as

they said the magical words:
"Friendship Forest!"

Instantly, a little door
appeared in the tree trunk.
The girls and Goldie squeezed
through, and Lily and Jess felt
themselves shrinking, just a
little. Then they were back in
Friendship Forest!

"Hello, girls," smiled Goldie. "It's my birthday today, and I wanted to invite you to come to my party!"

"Happy birthday!" the girls cried, hugging their friend.

The friends set off through the forest. Soon they reached Goldie's grotto, which was decorated beautifully.

A voice called, "Hello! We've come to see the birthday cat."

"It's the Sparklepaws!" Goldie cried happily.

There stood a family of cats.

Amelia was
the smallest
kitten.
She had
shining
blue
eyes and
white fur.
She handed Goldie
a pretty present. "Happy
birthday!" she cried.

"Thank you, Amelia," smiled
Goldie.

Lots of other animal friends
started to arrive.

Suddenly, a strange blue furry creature appeared, and stuffed some food into its mouth! Then it disappeared behind a large bush.

Behind the bush was a bouquet of flowers.

"They must be for Goldie," Lily said.

CHAPTER TWO

Trapped!

The bouquet was full of ugly grey flowers that smelled horrid.

Goldie opened the card that came with the flowers. It said:

Goldie,

Wishing you a HORRIBLE birthday!

Grizelda

"Grizelda is so mean!" cried Lily, horrified.

Grizelda was a wicked witch. She wanted to make all the animals leave Friendship Forest so she could have it all for herself!

Just then, the flowers began to grow.

"They're opening," cried Jess. The flowers looked

like big, hungry mouths!

"Keep back!" yelled Goldie.
But it was too late.

The biggest flower dived
towards Amelia. The kitten
gave a squeal as the mouth
snapped shut around her.

"Help!" mewed Amelia from
inside the flower.

"Those are snapdragons,"
Mrs Muddlepup gasped.
"They're impossible to
 open!"

Hermia, a friendly butterfly, fluttered over. "We sprinkle sugarsap on flowers that won't open," she said. "There's lots of sugarsap in Butterfly Bower!"

"Let's collect some and bring it back," Jess said.

Hermia gave the friends a shrinking violet flower to eat. They shrank to the size of butterflies

and climbed
into the tiny
bower to collect the
sugarsap.

Then Hermia gave
the girls growberry
blossoms to make them
grow bigger again.

"Time to free
Amelia!" cried
Goldie.

Back at the grotto, Lily,
Jess and Goldie sprinkled the
sugarsap liquid over the flowers.
But the bouquet shook the
sugarsap droplets off!

CHAPTER THREE

An Unwelcome Guest

"The sugarsap didn't work!" sobbed Mrs Sparklepaw.

"We're so sorry," Lily said.

Nobody knew what to do. Their plan had failed!

Jess gave a shout. She held up some leftover shrinking violets from her pocket.

"What if we feed these shrinking violets to the snapdragons? They'll shrink until they're too small to hold Amelia!" said Jess.

"Let's try it!" Lily cried.

Jess crept towards the bouquet. As soon as a flower lunged with its petals wide open, Jess tossed the shrinking violets deep inside the snapdragon's mouth.

Goldie and the girls watched as the flowers started to shake – and then shrink!

"It's working!" Lily cried as the bouquet got smaller. The flower opened, and out tumbled Amelia!

Lily darted forward to catch her, then Mrs Sparklepaw rushed over to give Amelia a big hug.

"Thank you for rescuing me!" cried Amelia.

"Now the birthday party can begin!" smiled Jess.

But a yellow-green orb of light was hurtling towards them. It  burst into a shower of smelly sparks. When they cleared, there stood Grizelda, her horrible face red with rage.

"You've stopped me this time!" she shrieked. "But this isn't the end!"

She snapped her fingers and disappeared.

Goldie smiled bravely. "We can't let Grizelda stop us from having fun. I'll go inside and get the party food ready."

A few minutes later the girls went to find Goldie. But there was no sign of their friend!

Lily gave a cry of horror. "Oh no," she said. "Grizelda must have taken her!"

PART TWO

Cat-napped!

CHAPTER FOUR

Where's Goldie?

Lily and Jess sat on Goldie's sofa, with Amelia Sparklepaw the kitten snuggled between them. They couldn't believe that the horrible witch had cat-napped Goldie!

When the other animals heard the news, they all gasped.

Amelia was staring at
something on the ground,
where Grizelda had been
standing. "Look," she said, "it's
a parasol leaf."

Lily's eyes shone with
excitement. "It must be a clue!"

"You're right!" cried Jess.
"If we can find where it came
from, maybe
it will help
us find
Goldie."

"There's
only one

parasol tree," trilled Hermia. "We'll take you there!"

Lily, Jess and Amelia started to follow the butterflies.

"Jess and I will look after Amelia," Lily called back to Mrs Sparklepaw as they left. "We promise!"

A while later the friends reached the parasol tree and searched all around, but there was nothing there.

"Look at that bush," Lily said, pointing. "There's something strange about it!"

As they drew nearer, they saw the bush was actually a building made of thick, thorny

branches all twisted together.

"This is exactly the sort of place where Grizelda would hide Goldie!" cried Jess.

"I'll find a way in," said Amelia. She wriggled forward on her tummy. "Look! Here's a nice big gap."

Lily and Jess crawled after the kitten. Fuzzy-skinned fruit hung from the bush. Lily knocked a fruits to the ground and it made an awful screeching sound!

Then they heard footsteps rushing towards them …

"Who's there?" Grizelda snarled.

"She won't find us!" Amelia said, touching the flower around her neck. "Hold my paws."

The girls held Amelia's paws, and immediately the three friends vanished.

CHAPTER FIVE

Grizelda's Gobbler

"This hiding hollyhock flower makes us invisible!" Amelia whispered to the girls.

Grizelda searched around but eventually she gave up, turned and walked away down the corridor, disappearing through a doorway.

Amelia and the girls were still invisible, so they crept through the door after Grizelda. Inside was the fluffy blue creature they'd seen outside Goldie's Grotto! Grizelda was feeding him leaves and twigs.

"You're going to help me take over the forest, little Gobbler!" she cackled.

The witch held up a glass jar.

Inside was a tuft of golden fur!

"Ha haaa!" sneered Grizelda. "Now I have Goldie's fur I just need to collect one more ingredient and I'll be ready to make my new potion. Friendship Forest will be mine!"

Lily looked quickly at Grizelda's notepad and saw that the last ingredient she needed for the potion was something called a shower flower.

Jess, Lily and Amelia crept out of the room. The hiding hollyhock magic wore off and they became visible again.

"Do you know where the shower flowers grow, Amelia?" asked Lily.

The kitten shook her fluffy head sadly. "I've never even heard of them."

The friends pushed open the next door and there was Goldie! Her paws were tied up with thick vines.

"I knew you'd come," Goldie

cried. "You're all so brave."

The girls tried to undo the vines, but the knots were too tough.

Just then the friends heard a pattering sound. Around the bend, padding on his big yellow paws, came Gobbler!

CHAPTER SIX

Rescue

When they reached Goldie's Grotto, Jess told everyone about Grizelda's potion.

"Whenever it rains, the shower flower grows at the spot where the first raindrop falls,"

explained Mrs Featherbill.

Goldie looked at the sky. "Why don't you all stay for a sleepover? We can search for a shower flower tomorrow!"

Everyone agreed. Goldie smiled at her friends. "Grizelda tried to spoil my birthday, but it's still been very special – because you're all here!"

PART THREE
Greedy Gobbler

CHAPTER SEVEN

The Dropper Spotter

Lily and Jess woke up early the next morning.

"We've still got to stop Grizelda making her horrid potion," whispered Lily.

The girls didn't know what the potion was for, but they knew it would be something awful!

Jess woke the others. "Time to get up. We have to stop Grizelda from finding a shower flower!" Amelia nodded eagerly.

Goldie opened the door and Jess pointed to some grey clouds floating high above the trees. "Hopefully it will rain later and a shower flower will grow somewhere!"

Lily looked thoughtful. "If a shower flower does grow today, how will we find it before Grizelda does?"

"Let's ask Mr Cleverfeather if he has an invention that can help us," said Jess.

The girls, Goldie and Amelia set off to visit Mr Cleverfeather the owl in his treetop home.

He hooted happily when he saw them.

Once he'd heard what the problem was, Mr Cleverfeather rummaged through his inventions. Eventually he produced a contraption rather like a watering can.

"This is a Dropper Spotter," said Mr Cleverfeather. "It detects raindrops."

"Hooray!" said Lily. "Now we can find the exact place where the shower flower will grow."

They thanked their owl friend and headed out into the

forest.

Jess started up the Dropper Spotter and it started to spin. Then it rose up into the air and zoomed away.

Lily picked Amelia up, and they all hurried after the Dropper Spotter.

As they pushed through the bushes, the kitten's ears twitched. "Stop!" she said. "Someone is calling for help!"

The voice seemed to be coming from a bush. Lily grabbed the Dropper Spotter, so it wouldn't get too far ahead.

There was a sudden explosion of sparks and there stood Grizelda, with Gobbler tucked under her arm!

CHAPTER EIGHT

The Shower Flower

With a cackle, Grizelda
snatched the Dropper Spotter
from Lily.

"Now I'll find the shower
flower!" she crowed.

She pressed the Dropper
Spotter's start button and it
whizzed into the air.

The four friends raced after Grizelda. Soon they reached a large clearing. There stood Grizelda and Gobbler with the Dropper Spotter.

Just then a single raindrop fell from a cloud and splashed on to the ground at Grizelda's feet. Instantly, a green shoot sprang up and began to grow. When it was as tall as Grizelda, a huge blue flower burst into bloom.

Lily gasped when she saw it. "The shower flower!" she cried. "Quick, let's get it."

They raced towards the tall
plant, but they were too late.
Grizelda plucked the flower
and stuffed it into her flask. She
gave a mean smile. "Aha! My
potion is complete!"

Goldie, Amelia and the girls watched helplessly as the potion bubbled.

Grizelda poured the liquid on to a handful of leaves and gave them to Gobbler.

"Eeeeeep!" he squeaked and began eating.

Jess gave a cry. "He's getting bigger!"

They watched as the furry blue creature grew larger. He

bounded to a nearby bush and quickly munched his way through it, still growing.

"He's going to get big enough to eat up the entire forest!" Grizelda cackled. "He'll gobble up everything – including the animals' homes! In a few hours, Friendship Forest will be mine!"

Grizelda cackled and vanished in a burst of sparks.

"Oh, I wish we could make Gobbler smaller somehow, like we did with the snapdragons," Lily cried.

"We can! I know where the shrinking violets grow!" Amelia said excitedly.

The girls quickly picked lots of shrinking violets and rushed back to Gobbler. He was enormous now!

The friends tried to feed him the shrinking violets, but he refused to eat them.

CHAPTER NINE

One Last Surprise

Gobbler looked over the girls' shoulders. "EEP!" he boomed.

"He's spotted the Treasure Tree!" cried Lily. "We have to stop him from eating it."

As Gobbler set off for the Treasure Tree, Jess yelled, "I've got an idea!"

Jess pulled out her sketchbook and pencil and scribbled a little message. Then she asked one of the butterflies to give the note to Mr Cleverfeather.

The four friends followed Gobbler to the Treasure Tree. There was Grizelda – encouraging Gobbler to eat everything!

Mr Cleverfeather appeared overhead. He was carrying the Blitzer, an invention that whizzed everything together.

Jess stuffed the shrinking

violets into the Blitzer, and Lily
added twigs and leaves. They
whizzed them into a purple
liquid.

"Here's a delicious drink for
you, Gobbler!" Lily called.

The great furry creature
opened his
mouth
happily
and Jess
poured
the
drink
inside.

Gobbler instantly shrank down to being small again.

Grizelda was furious. "You've won this time," she shrieked, "but one day Friendship Forest will be mine!" And she was gone in a shower of sparks.

Now Goldie could enjoy her birthday party. Gobbler joined in with the fun.

"Mum says he can live with us," said Amelia. "He can eat all the weeds in the garden!"

Soon it was time for the girls to go home. Goldie took

them to the Friendship Tree. "I'll never forget my exciting birthday!" she said.

The girls stepped through the doorway into Brightley Meadow.

"What an amazing adventure," smiled Lily.

"Yes," agreed Jess. "Who knows what will happen next with our magic animal friends!"

The End